NATASHA WING'S
The Night Before
Kindergarten Graduation

Grosset & Dunlap

Thank you to Krista Crumrine's kindergartners
and all the teachers, parents, and kids
who offered ideas—NW

To Olivia, kindergarten graduate extraordinaire,
and to AJ, Eloise, Louie, and Rocco,
future first-rate alumni—AW

GROSSET & DUNLAP
An Imprint of Penguin Random House LLC, New York

Text copyright © 2019 by Natasha Wing. Illustrations copyright © 2019 by Penguin Random House LLC. All rights reserved.
Published by Grosset & Dunlap, an imprint of Penguin Random House LLC, New York.
GROSSET & DUNLAP is a trademark of Penguin Random House LLC.
Manufactured in China.

Visit us online at www.penguinrandomhouse.com.

Library of Congress Cataloging-in-Publication Data is available upon request.

ISBN 9781524790011   10 9 8 7 6 5 4 3 2 1

NATASHA WING'S
The Night Before
Kindergarten
Graduation

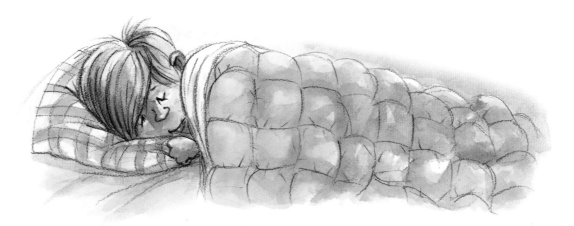

By Natasha Wing
Illustrated by Amy Wummer

Grosset & Dunlap

'Twas the night before graduation.
School had flown by so fast!
Kids prepared for their big day
that would be here at last.

Oodles of art projects were displayed on the wall.
The very first ones had been made back in fall.

At home the kids practiced
their graduation song.

Most sang it in key—
no one got the words wrong.

Some went over their steps
for tomorrow's cool dance.
Sam slid across the floor
and split his sweatpants!

Kate got her hair trimmed.
Her bangs were now straight.

Jorge made a card saying, "Miss Sunrise, you're great!"

Clean outfits were hung
in their closets with care.
Sneakers or sandals?
Oh, which pair to wear?

Kids flipped and they flopped about in their beds, while visions of kindergarten danced in their heads.

Then before they knew it—
it was graduation day!
Would their teacher miss them?
Would their friends move away?

Parents dropped off their kids.
"We'll see you in a while."
Miss Sunrise greeted her class
with a slightly sad smile.

"Are you ready?" she asked.
The kids shouted, "Let's go!"
So they put on their caps
for their graduation show.

When what to their wonder-struck eyes should appear,
but a gym full of families—everyone was here!
The stage—how festive! The lights—so bright!
Some kids started getting a touch of stage fright.

The kindergartners performed
to a proud, beaming crowd.

People stood up and clapped
as the children all bowed.

The ceremony wrapped up
with a favorite song.

Parents knew it, too,
so they all sang along!

Miss Sunrise cut into the cake
and said to everyone,
"This year was amazing—
look at all that you've done!"

The kids were excited for summer
but sad saying goodbye.
Miss Sunrise wished them well.
Was a tear in her eye?

The whole class had loved
the fun memories they'd made.
Kindergarten was great.
Now it's on to first grade!